Holidays

Ramadan

by R.J. Bailey

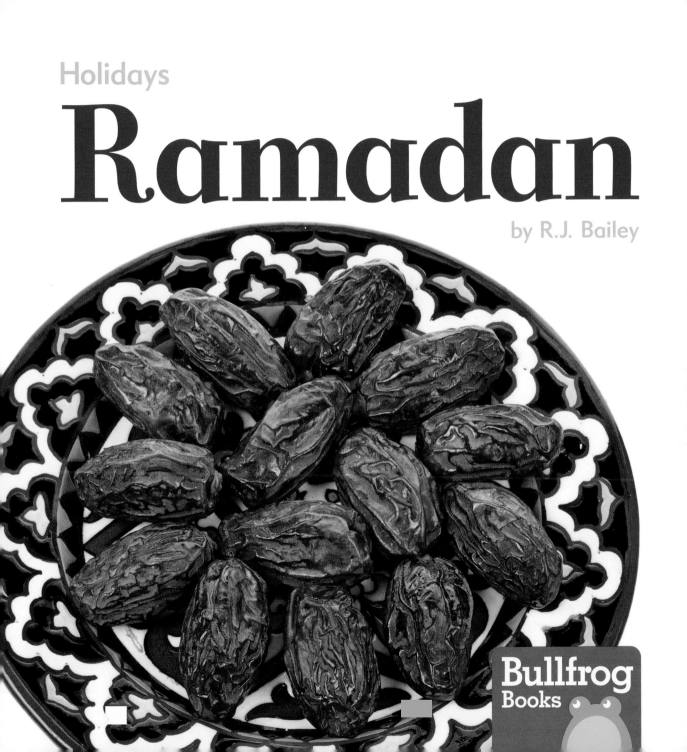

Bullfrog Books

Ideas for Parents and Teachers

Bullfrog Books let children practice reading informational text at the earliest reading levels. Repetition, familiar words, and photo labels support early readers.

Before Reading

- Discuss the cover photo. What does it tell them?

- Look at the picture glossary together. Read and discuss the words.

Read the Book

- "Walk" through the book and look at the photos. Let the child ask questions. Point out the photo labels.

- Read the book to the child, or have him or her read independently.

After Reading

- Prompt the child to think more. Ask: Does your family observe Ramadan? What sorts of things do you see when people observe Ramadan?

Bullfrog Books are published by Jump!
5357 Penn Avenue South
Minneapolis, MN 55419
www.jumplibrary.com

Library of Congress Cataloging-in-Publication Data

Names: Bailey, R.J., author.
Title: Ramadan / by R.J. Bailey.
Description: Minneapolis, MN: Jump!, [2016]
Series: Holidays | Includes index.
"K to grade 3, ages 5–8"—ECIP data view.
Identifiers: LCCN 2016007920 (print)
LCCN 2016008541 (ebook)
ISBN 9781620313572 (hard cover: alk. paper)
ISBN 9781624964046 (e-book)
Subjects: LCSH: Ramadan—Juvenile literature.
Fasts and feasts—Islam—Juvenile literature.
Classification: LCC BP186.4 .B35 2016 (print)
LCC BP186.4 (ebook) | DDC 297.3/62—dc23
LC record available at http://lccn.loc.gov/2016007920

Editor: Kirsten Chang
Series Designer: Ellen Huber
Book Designer: Michelle Sonnek
Photo Researchers: Kirsten Chang & Michelle Sonnek

Photo Credits: All photos by Shutterstock except:
Adobe Stock, 14–15; Alamy, 9, 16–17.

Printed in the United States of America at Corporate Graphics in North Mankato, Minnesota.

Table of Contents

What Is Ramadan?

Ramadan is a
Muslim holiday.

It lasts one month.

5

When is it?

The ninth month
of the Muslim year.

It begins when we
see the new moon.

It is a time to show faith.
We fast. We pray.

We help those in need.

When the sun is up,
we do not eat.

We do not drink.

We visit the mosque.

Sam prays.

mosque

13

Lulu reads a book.

God sent it to us.

It is called the Koran.

The sun sets.

The fast ends.

Mom makes food.

Yum! We are hungry.

The month is over.
We give gifts.

18

What does Ali get?

Money!

19

We hang lights.

We eat sweets.

Happy Ramadan!

Symbols of Ramadan

new moon

gifts

sweets

lights

Picture Glossary

faith
Strong belief in the existence of God.

mosque
A place where Muslims worship.

Koran
The holy book of Islam, one of the largest religions in the world.

Muslim
A person who follows the Islam religion.

Index

To Learn More

Learning more is as easy as 1, 2, 3.

1) Go to www.factsurfer.com

2) Enter "Ramadan" into the search box.

3) Click the "Surf" button to see a list of websites.

With factsurfer.com, finding more information is just a click away.